Sit on My C

by Matthew Damon   illustrated by Wallace Keller

Orlando Boston Dallas Chicago San Diego

Visit *The Learning Site!*

www.harcourtschool.com

ISBN 0-15-325415-7

8 9 10 121 10 09 08 07 06 05 04

Ordering Options
ISBN 0-15-323766-X (Collection)
ISBN 0-15-329534-1 (package of 5)

Sit on my brown chair.

 Sit on my red chair.

Sit on my blue chair.

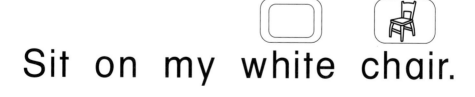

Sit on my white chair.

Sit on my purple chair.

Sit on my  pink chair.

I fit on my chair.